Aunt Nell arrives.

So now Emily had Aunt Nell wrapped around her finger, too, along with the others, before I'd even had a chance to meet her. I made a list in my mind of all the things I wanted to happen to Emily, from being eaten by cannibals to burning at the stake. I was used to Emily's back-stabbing treachery, but this time she had gone too far.

Mama said the Good Book says I must forgive my sister not seven times but seventy times seven and "Vengeance is mine" sayeth the Lord. So sitting there by the quarry, I resigned myself to burning for all eternity in the fires of hell, for I surely could not find it in my heart to forgive her.

So deep was I in self-pity and vengeance seeking that I did not hear the footsteps, and I nearly jumped out of my skin when a hand was placed on my shoulder. I twisted around and looked into the smiling face of the woman I'd seen in our yard.

"You must be Lily," said Aunt Nell.

∽∾

"Readers will identify with [Lily's] frustration, sibling rivalry, and ultimately her pain. . . . [An] engaging coming-of-age story."   —*School Library Journal*

OTHER BOOKS BY NATALIE KINSEY-WARNOCK

As Long as There Are Mountains
The Canada Geese Quilt
The Night the Bells Rang

If Wishes Were Horses

If Wishes Were Horses

NATALIE KINSEY-WARNOCK

PUFFIN BOOKS

PUFFIN BOOKS
Published by the Penguin Group
Penguin Putnam Books for Young Readers,
345 Hudson Street, New York, New York 10014, U.S.A.
Penguin Books Ltd, 80 Strand, London WC2R ORL, England
Penguin Books Australia Ltd, Ringwood, Victoria, Australia
Penguin Books Canada Ltd, 10 Alcorn Avenue, Toronto, Ontario, Canada M4V 3B2
Penguin Books (N.Z.) Ltd, 182-190 Wairau Road, Auckland 10, New Zealand

Penguin Books Ltd, Registered Offices: Harmondsworth, Middlesex, England

First published in the United States of America by Dutton Children's Books,
a division of Penguin Putnam Books for Young Readers, 2000
Published by Puffin Books,
a division of Penguin Putnam Books for Young Readers, 2002

1 3 5 7 9 10 8 6 4 2

CIP DATA IS AVAILABLE UPON REQUEST FROM THE LIBRARY OF CONGRESS.

Puffin Books ISBN 0-14-230143-4

Printed in the United States of America

For Shawn and Jerry

When the gods wish to punish us,
they answer our prayers.

—Oscar Wilde

If Wishes Were Horses

1

My great-grandfather often talked about his ghost pains. He'd lost a leg at Gettysburg, but, right up until the day he died, he said that missing limb ached and itched as if it were still attached to him. I didn't understand then—how could you feel something that was gone?—but now I know what he meant. I have ghost pains, too, but my pains are for a whole person. Some days it seems as if she's still here, and I let myself pretend, just for a moment, that what happened that summer was just a bad dream.

The summer of 1932 began like any other summer. Even though we were smack dab in the middle of the Depression, things here in northern Vermont were pretty much as they'd been all along. It's been said that most Vermonters didn't realize times were so hard during the Depression since they never knew them to be all that good beforehand, and there is truth in that. Most folks up here in this hard country never had a lot to begin with, including us, but we had our farm and raised our own food, so we were better off than most. Emily and I helped Mama with the washing every Monday, the ironing every Tuesday, and the baking every Saturday. In between, we had to keep the corn weeded and pick beetles off the potato plants. Emily especially hated that, seeing as she's so squeamish about spiders and insects and such, which I am not. We had the same chores day after day, week after week—the same kind of summer I'd always known. Until Great-aunt Nell came to visit.

Before that summer, Emily and I didn't even know Grandma had a sister. Oh, I suppose Grandma may have mentioned her once or twice, but Emily and I had just never paid much attention, probably because we were too busy fighting. Emily and I almost never talked to each other; we argued. Just because she was one year older, Emily thought she could boss me around day and night.

"It's your turn to get the cows," Emily would say, even if it wasn't. Or "Lily May Randall, you go out and weed the carrots," or some such thing until I was mad enough to spit.

We even fought about animals. Papa had been raised on a farm, but Mama had not. She hadn't grown up with animals and was still timid around them, so she'd never allowed us to have pets, but that didn't keep us from arguing about them. Emily wanted a cat, but I loved horses and wanted one for my very own. Papa had three horses: Bob and Joe, the giant workhorses, and Lady, his driving mare, but he wouldn't let Emily or me near them. They were all as gentle as lambs, even Lady who had plenty of spirit, but Papa said you never can tell. Papa's own daddy had been killed when a horse kicked him in the head, so I guess he's got good reason to be cautious, but I still think it's not fair. I can't ride them or even pat them. I mean, you can die from choking on a piece of bread or meat, but that doesn't mean you're not gonna eat, does it?

I mostly don't think life is fair anyway. Ever since I can remember, I've loved horses. I've got pictures of them hanging up on my wall, and I've read *Black Beauty* a zillion times. That's the kind of horse I want—a black one like Black Beauty. Every one of my birthdays, and every Christmas, I've begged for a horse, but Mama says "No, not this year" or "No, not until you're older," but it all means no, not ever. Then last week, Emily found a little half-starved kitten that somebody dumped off at our place, and Mama said she could keep it.

I flew into a rage over that and was sent to Emily's and my room without any supper. How I hated Emily that night. I even hated the kitten. I sat and let my feelings fester all night and was still stewing when I confronted Mama in the morning.

"Having a cat is not the same as a horse,"

Mama said as she sent me off to our room again, but I know it's only because she loves Emily more than me. They all do—Mama, Papa, even Grandma, though they'd never admit it. Emily's always been the favored one, and my only consolation that day in my room was that Emily had to beat the rugs and mop the floor all by herself.

"It's time you grew up," Mama also said to me, and I did not tell her that is what I most want to do. When I am grown, I will have one hundred horses if I want, and I will live as far away from Emily as I can.

2

The first thing that promised to lift that summer out of the ordinary was the circus to be held at the Lyndonville Fairgrounds, some twenty-five miles away. Every year we went to the Orleans County Fair and saw horse races and cattle judging and horse pulling and got to eat cotton candy, but we'd never been to a circus. Posters were tacked up all over the countryside, on barns and trees and telephone poles, all with bright pictures and large letters announcing tigers and elephants and the man who ate fire. Of course, Emily and I argued about what we wanted to see.

"The lions are the best," Emily said.

"No, the monkeys are the best," I said, though we had never seen lions or monkeys, either, except in books.

"You would like them," Emily said. "You look just like one."

I yanked Emily's hair, and she screamed. She's such a baby that way. Grandma came running.

"Lily! Emily! Stop that this instant!" she said. "You ought to be ashamed, two grown girls like yourselves."

"She pulled some of my hair out!" Emily cried, rubbing her head, and two big teardrops filled her eyes. I swear, Emily could make her eyes well up at the drop of a hat.

"She started it!" I yelled.

Grandma sighed.

"I declare, you girls could argue about which was the sun and which was the moon," she said. "I don't see why you can't get along."

"Because she's mean and bossy," I told her, glaring at Emily, who glared right back.

"In my day," Grandma said, ignoring us both, "my sister and I were the best of friends. We never had a bit of trouble between us."

Now Emily and I stared at Grandma.

"You have a sister?" Emily said.

"What's her name?" I asked.

"Why, I'm surprised at you," Grandma said. "I know I've told you girls before about your great-aunt Nell. She's been all over the world."

"Why haven't we ever seen her?" I asked.

"She's been a missionary in India for the past twenty years," Grandma said. "She came home for a visit twelve years ago, when Emily was just a baby, but I haven't seen her since. I miss her."

"Do you ever hear from her?" Emily asked.

"I write to her every month, but I guess she's too busy to answer. Every now and then, she jots me a couple of sentences," Grandma said. "Nell's not much of a letter writer."

That evening, after chores and supper, Emily and I lugged the heavy atlas to the kitchen table and pulled the kerosene lamp close. We carefully turned the pages until we came to the map of India.

"Do you know where she is?" Emily asked Grandma.

Grandma, bent over a piece of lace she was tatting, looked up, startled.

"Who?" she asked.

"Your sister. Where is she in India?" I asked, impatiently.

"Nell?" Grandma said, and studied the ceiling. "Let's see. It's been a long time since I've heard from her, and she could be working someplace else by now, but the last I knew she was in some place called Batala."

The names of the villages were so small, and India so large, that twenty minutes passed before Emily and I located Batala in the northern part of India, near the border of Pakistan. We tried to imagine what life there was like, but we could not.

"I wonder what it looks like there," Emily said.

"I wonder what Aunt Nell eats," I said. "And what she wears and what the people look like and how they get from place to place."

"When I grow up, I'm going to travel all over the world," Emily said.

"Me, too," I said. "I'm going to climb mountains and explore rivers and go to the North Pole."

"It's too cold there," Emily said. "I'm going to Africa instead, where I can see lions and zebras and giraffes in the wild. And I'm going to ride an elephant."

"Right now, the two of you are going to bed," Grandma said.

My dreams that night were filled with images of snake charmers and sacred cows and images of a tall woman riding a camel across a desert.

Perhaps Aunt Nell sensed we were thinking about her, because two weeks later, Papa brought a letter from town. It read:

Dear Edna,
I am coming for a visit. I shall be arriving in Barton on Friday on the morning train.

Your loving sister,
Nell

Grandma was right, I thought. Aunt Nell wasn't much of a letter writer.

"Gracious!" Grandma said. "That's tomorrow! How will we ever get ready in time?"

Grandma set everyone to work: Mama made rhubarb pies (Aunt Nell's favorite). Papa blacked the stove and whitewashed the pantry. Emily beat the rugs, and I polished the silver until I got a blister, but I didn't mind. Just when it seemed that nothing out of the ordinary ever happened here, now there were two exciting things to look forward to.

"Won't it be fun having Aunt Nell here?" Emily asked, her eyes sparkling.

I nodded and thought of all the places Aunt Nell had seen.

"I bet she has a hundred stories to tell," I said.

"Now, don't go tiring Aunt Nell with all your questions," Grandma said. "She's going to need to rest after her long trip."

"She can rest while we go to the circus," I said.

Mama brushed her hair back from her forehead.

"I hate to disappoint you girls, but I'm afraid you won't be able to go to the circus."

Emily and I couldn't believe our ears.

"But, Mama, we have to go," I wailed.

"Don't carry on so, Lily," Mama said. "I'm sorry, but your father has hay to get in, and Grandma and I will be busy with Aunt Nell."

"Maybe Aunt Nell would like to go to the circus, too," Emily said, and for once, I thought she had a good idea.

"I should say not," Grandma said. "I'm sure the only thing Nell wants is some peace and quiet."

Emily and I sulked all afternoon, which is unusual for Emily. Usually, she acts like such a Miss Goody Two-Shoes, but it is only an act she puts on for Mama, Papa, and Grandma. When they are not around, she is as stubborn and selfish as I am.

Mama scolded both of us for being childish and plunked us down in the pantry to help prepare supper. As soon as she left the room, I slapped down my paring knife.

"I'm going to ask Papa if I can ride to town

with him to pick up Aunt Nell at the train station," I said. I knew as soon as I said it that I should have kept my mouth shut and not given Emily any ideas.

"Oh no, you're not," Emily said, stomping her foot. "You're going to stay here and help me peel potatoes."

"Am not!" I yelled and shot for the door, but I ran headlong into Grandma, who was carrying a bowl of succotash. The bowl crashed to the floor, and succotash flew everywhere.

"I declare, I never saw two sisters fight so," Grandma said as we scooped up handfuls of corn and beans and mopped up the milk. "I want you to be on your best behavior while Nell is here, especially you, Lily. You two are going to act like young ladies, do you hear me?"

We nodded meekly, and Grandma went back into the kitchen, muttering as she went.

Emily and I looked at each other. Everything had gone wrong. We wouldn't be going to the circus, and now Aunt Nell's visit didn't sound like any fun either.

Still, I had a plan I intended to carry out. If I could go with Papa to pick up Aunt Nell, I'd be so charming and vivacious that Aunt Nell would love me instantly. We would have so much in common, for in my heart, I am an adventurer like she is. I would win her so completely that Emily would forever pale in comparison. I imagined how Aunt Nell would ask me to the circus, and she'd buy a horse for me just to please me, and I would be the one she'd share secrets with. She might even invite me to travel the world with her, so fond of my company she'd become. For once, I would be first in someone's heart.

Papa didn't come home for supper.

"The cows were out in Clyde Lafont's field, so he's repairing fence," Mama explained. "We'll just go ahead and eat, and I'll heat up something for him later."

I lay awake, listening for the thud of Papa's boots on the porch. As soon as I heard it, I would sneak downstairs and ask him, but by the time he came home, long past dark, I was dreaming dreams of my travels with Aunt Nell.

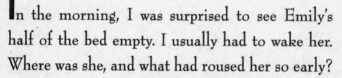

3

In the morning, I was surprised to see Emily's half of the bed empty. I usually had to wake her. Where was she, and what had roused her so early?

"Lily, eat your breakfast, then wash up these dishes as quickly as you can," Mama said. "There's already water hot on the stove."

"It's Emily's turn to wash the dishes," I said, wondering why Emily was dressed in her Sunday best.

"Emily's going with your papa to pick up Aunt Nell, so you'll do them today," Mama said.

I glared at Emily, hoping I could poison her with my eyes, but she wouldn't look at me.

"Can't I go, too?" I asked, but I already knew the answer.

"I need one of you girls to help me pick and shell peas, and Emily already asked Papa this morning."

I felt my skin turn cold. So that's why she'd gotten up so early. Such treachery. My hand began twitching, so strong was my desire to slap her. I would have, too, if Mama hadn't stood there.

Unable to eat, I pushed my oatmeal around in its bowl while Emily scurried about with last-minute preparations. As she pranced out the door, she stuck out her tongue at me. I stuck out my tongue, too, just as Mama turned to tell me to stop dawdling.

"That's enough of that, Lily," she said. "I'm ashamed of your behavior. When are you going to grow up?"

I started to protest, to say that Emily had started it, but Mama raised her hand.

"I don't want to hear it. Emily doesn't control

your behavior; you do. I'll have none of it while Aunt Nell is here. Understood?"

Silence.

"Lily." Mama's voice was icy. "Is that understood?"

It is difficult to speak when one's teeth are clenched, but I managed to say, "Yes, Mama." Arguing with Mama would get me nowhere. My time would be better spent plotting revenge on Emily.

After I'd washed the dishes, swept the floor and picked and shelled what seemed like a zillion peas, Mama sent me out to pick a bouquet of daisies and wild iris. She set them on the table and surveyed the room, nodding approval.

"Now, run put on your Sunday dress," she said to me. "We don't want Aunt Nell thinking you're a tomboy."

"But I am a tomboy," I said.

Mama sighed.

"Lily, just do as I ask," she said.

As I climbed the stairs to Emily's and my room, I heard her say to Grandma, "Did you ever meet such an obstreperous child?" and Grandma's soft laugh.

"She is obstinate, all right," Grandma said.

Obstinate I know; it means stubborn and mulish. But *obstreperous*? I rolled the word around with my tongue, liking the sound of it, and reminded myself to look it up in the dictionary. I thought it a lovely word, and I was pleased Mama used it on me.

I opened the closet and looked at my dress with loathing. It was cut from a dress of Mama's to fit Emily and then handed down to me. It was an ugly print to begin with, and it had not gotten prettier with age, but even had it been the most beautiful dress I'd ever seen, still I would not have wanted to put it on. I hated dresses. Emily, of course, loved nothing more than to don frilly clothes and preen in front of a mirror. Just last week she'd gotten invited to a birthday party for one of the town girls, and she'd begged and begged for a new dress. Mama had used the money she'd saved for new shoes for herself to buy material for Emily, while I had to be content with homely hand-me-downs.

I was struggling with the buttons (for the hundredth time I vowed that if I ever found the man—and I am certain it must be a man—who designed dresses that button up the back, I would boil him in oil), when I heard the buggy pull up in the dooryard.

Drat, I'd wanted to be out there to greet Aunt Nell the moment she arrived. Hope still flickered in me that I could charm Aunt Nell and she would see in me a kindred spirit. But when I looked out the window and saw a tall woman step from the buggy, her arm around Emily and both of them laughing, my hope died, leaving something dark and empty within me. It was not unusual for me to hate Emily, for I did it often, but suddenly I hated Aunt Nell, too.

I ripped the dress from me, yanking my coveralls back on. I ran down the stairs and out the back door where no one could see me, running with all my might to the old quarry that had been carved out of the hill a half-mile above our farm.

The quarry, long abandoned and filled with water, was my place of refuge. It was my place and my place alone, for Emily did not go there. I told her there were snakes, even though there were not, and spiders, which there were though I exaggerated their size. It was my place to think and dream, and very often it was my place to plan how I would get back at Emily.

So now she had Aunt Nell wrapped around her finger, too, along with the others, before I'd even had a chance to meet her. I made a list in my mind of all the things I wanted to happen to Emily, from being eaten by cannibals to burning at the stake. I was used to Emily's back-stabbing treachery, but this time she had gone too far.

Mama said the Good Book says I must forgive my sister not seven times but seventy times seven and "Vengeance is mine" sayeth the Lord. So sitting there by the quarry, I resigned myself to burning for all eternity in the fires of hell, for I surely could not find it in my heart to forgive her.

So deep was I in self-pity and vengeance seeking that I did not hear the footsteps, and I nearly jumped out of my skin when a hand was placed on my shoulder. I twisted around and looked into the smiling face of the woman I'd seen in our yard.

"You must be Lily," she said.

4

"**H**ow did you find me?" was all I could think to say when I found my tongue.

"This was my hideout when I was a girl," Aunt Nell said. "I spent many afternoons here, thinking and dreaming. And swimming."

"You were allowed to swim here?" I asked, feeling the all-too-familiar sting of envy. I was forbidden to swim in the quarry. That didn't keep me from doing it, but I always felt guilty after I had.

"Of course not," Aunt Nell said. "That was part of the attraction."

In spite of myself, I smiled. It was going to be difficult to continue hating Aunt Nell; she and I had so much in common.

Aunt Nell settled in beside me, and for the first time I noticed she was wearing pants. Pants! Women of Aunt Nell's age just did not wear pants. It was thought scandalous.

Aunt Nell saw my look of astonishment.

"Don't you just hate wearing dresses?" she asked. "Pants are ever so much more comfortable. And practical, too."

My breath caught in my throat. Kindred spirits.

"But they are hot in the summer," she said. "Let's go swimming."

"I forgot my bathing suit," I said. I didn't add that I wasn't allowed.

"Me, too," Aunt Nell said and shocked me by stripping off her clothes and diving into the quarry, stark naked. I sat there, my mouth hanging open until Aunt Nell splashed me.

"You look hot, too," she said. "Come on in."

My ears burning red, I turned my back to her and undressed as quickly as I could. I jumped in, yelping as I hit the cold water.

Later, as we lay drying on the rocks, Aunt Nell looked beyond the quarry to the green hills and fields that surrounded us and sighed contentedly.

"I'm so glad to be back," she said. "I've missed Vermont so. And Edna." She squeezed my hand.

"I've missed watching you and Emily grow up, too. You and Emily are every bit as pretty as your grandma said you were."

In all her letters to Aunt Nell, the one word I was sure Grandma had *not* used to describe me was pretty. Maybe Grandma had written "petty," and Aunt Nell had misread it. But since Aunt Nell had brought up her name, I felt I might as well let her know up front where I stood on the issue of Emily.

"I can't stand her," I said. "She's mean and sneaky, and she's not near so good as she makes herself out to be. And she's bossy to boot."

Aunt Nell laughed.

"That's what I used to say about Edna," she

said. "She was always telling me what to do. We fought like cats and dogs."

"You did? Grandma said you never had a bit of trouble between you."

"Edna said *that*?" Aunt Nell exclaimed. "Why, that's not how it was at all. She threw my best hat in the pigpen, put tacks in my shoes, and once she hid a hen in my bed. You don't know what surprise is until you've sat on a chicken! I was afraid to go to bed for weeks."

I burst out laughing.

"I bet the chicken was surprised, too," I said, and that made Aunt Nell laugh.

"Did Grandma really do that?" I had to ask. I couldn't imagine Grandma being so mean.

"She sure did," Aunt Nell said. "Of course, I did a few things to her, too. I cut up her hair ribbons, put pepper in her pudding and a toad in her underwear drawer."

Emily's reaction to frogs and toads was pretty much the same as it was for anything that crawled, slithered, or flew, and I made another mental note to find a toad for Emily's underwear drawer.

"You must have really hated Grandma," I said.

"Hated Edna? Not at all," Aunt Nell said. "Oh, at times I guess I did. But really she was my best friend."

It didn't sound like best friends to me.

"But what about the chicken in bed? And the toad?" I asked.

"Oh, that. We just got angry at each other."

"Well, I'm angry at Emily most of the time," I said. "And I do hate her."

Aunt Nell didn't say anything, and I felt like kicking myself. Here I had Aunt Nell all to myself, and I was talking about Emily, my least favorite subject. I wanted to hear about India and all of Aunt Nell's travels.

Before I could ask any questions, we heard the dinner bell ring. We reached for our clothes, and I giggled, thinking how Grandma would be shocked to learn Aunt Nell and I had been skinny-dipping.

"You know," I said, "you're not at all the way Grandma made you out to be."

5

Next morning, while he waited for the dew to dry so he could mow some more, Papa said he would drive Aunt Nell around the countryside and show her all the changes in the twelve years since she'd visited (though I myself could not think of one solitary thing that had changed). And since I'd done Emily's work when she and Papa had gone to pick up Aunt Nell, Mama said Emily would do my work so I could go with them. Emily was all set to pitch a fit, but when I whispered to her my plan to somehow ask Aunt Nell to take us to the circus, she nodded happily.

We drove to West Glover, then down the steep,

winding hill to Glover and climbed again up toward Stone Pond, Lady's smooth road-trot eating up the miles. I kept hoping Aunt Nell would notice the circus announcements and offer to take us, but she was too busy chattering away with Papa about who lived where and what so-and-so's son was doing now. Once, I cleared my throat to point out a bright poster of tigers, but Papa gave me a warning glance, and I held my tongue.

We had just passed Stone Pond, a lovely place where Papa took us once or twice a year to picnic and swim, and still eight miles from home, when Lady stumbled and almost fell. Papa was out of the buggy and at her head before the buggy came to a stop. Mama says Papa's addlebrained when it comes to that horse.

"She's got a nail in her foot," Papa said, already beginning to unbuckle the harness. "I'll pull it out, but I'll still have to walk her home."

My heart sank. There went our plans for the circus. Even if I got Aunt Nell to agree to take us, now we had no way to get there.

"Who lives here?" Aunt Nell asked, pointing to a weathered farmhouse up ahead.

"Duncan Babcock," Papa answered.

"Couldn't you borrow a horse from him?"

"Word has it he got rid of his cows and horses and bought himself an automobile," Papa said.

"Would he lend that to us?" Aunt Nell asked.

"I doubt it," Papa said. "Babcock's never been one to help out his neighbors, but I'll see if he'll give you two a ride home while I walk Lady back."

Papa came back muttering under his breath.

"That blackhearted so-and-so won't help us at all," he said. I think Papa would have called Mr. Babcock something worse if Aunt Nell hadn't been there.

"I'll go over to George Kennison's and borrow a horse from him," Papa said.

Aunt Nell and I waited and waited and waited. I wondered what was keeping Papa.

"Well," Aunt Nell said, "we can't just sit here for the rest of the day. We've got to get home. I'm going to talk to Mr. Babcock," and she marched right up to his house.

I ran to keep up with her.

"Aunt Nell, have you ever driven an automobile?"

"Once," Aunt Nell said. "But the accident I was involved in was not my fault," which provoked my curiosity something awful.

When Mr. Babcock answered the door, Aunt Nell came right to the point.

"Mr. Babcock, we need to get home. I was wondering if we might borrow your automobile."

Mr. Babcock spat tobacco, just missing Aunt Nell's shoe. I didn't take that as a good sign.

"I already told Wesley I ain't about to let anybody borrow that car, least of all some woman."

Aunt Nell's eyes narrowed.

"I can assure you that I'm quite capable of driving your automobile," Aunt Nell said. I noticed she didn't mention anything about the accident that wasn't her fault.

"Nobody's borrowing that car," Mr. Babcock said. "And I ain't driving you home either."

"Well, do you have a horse we might use just to get home?"

"Ain't got no horse."

I tugged at Aunt Nell's sleeve.

"Yes, he does," I whispered.

"What's she saying?" Mr. Babcock asked, fixing his evil eye on me. I wanted to duck behind Aunt Nell, but I was getting riled at how Mr. Babcock was being so nasty. He'd always given me the willies the few times I'd seen him, but I figured if Aunt Nell could stand up to him, so could I.

"You do too have a horse," I said boldly. "I saw it behind your barn."

Mr. Babcock snorted.

"That old broken-down piece of horseflesh? Only thing he's good for now is the coyotes and crows. Fact is, Leon's coming to pick him up this afternoon."

Leon (short for Napoleon) Benoit ran the local slaughterhouse, and I despised him. Papa says Leon makes a living out of dying same as Mr. Calhoun, the undertaker, but it's an honest living, whereas Mr. Calhoun preys on people's grief and shames them into paying more for a burial than they can afford. Leastways, that's what Papa says, and when he recollects the point he's trying to make to me, he tells me I have to grow up (which I have heard before) and stop being so tender-hearted.

Growing up on a farm, I have witnessed the deaths of many animals: stillborn calves, chickens beheaded and readied for the cooking pot, cows struck by lightning, and butchering time when we do in the pig or bull we've tended so carefully up till then, but I have never gotten used to it. And standing on Mr. Babcock's porch, thinking of the fate of his horse, I shivered.

"Perhaps we could use the horse to get us home, and Leon could pick him up there," Aunt Nell said. She hopped off the porch. "Let's take a look at him," she said and headed for the barn without waiting for us.

"Hey, you ain't got no right to go snooping around here," Mr. Babcock yelled, running after her, but Aunt Nell paid him no mind.

I hurried after both of them. When I rounded the corner of the barn and set eyes on the horse, my breath caught in my throat.

Mr. Babcock's horse was the sorriest piece of horseflesh I had ever seen. His coat was so caked with mud and manure I could scarcely tell what color he was supposed to be, but I could see how his bones jutted out at all angles and the sores on his legs and back where he'd been whipped. He didn't even lift his head as we approached his enclosure where there was not one blade of grass in sight, or water, despite the day running hot. I wondered how he'd managed to stay alive.

Aunt Nell must have had the same thought.

"The poor thing," she breathed. "Death will be a blessing for that pitiful creature."

As much as I loved horses and despised Leon Benoit, I had to agree with Aunt Nell that putting down this horse was a kindness.

Aunt Nell spun on Mr. Babcock, and her eyes that had been so full of sympathy for the horse almost blazed sparks.

"And you, Mr. Babcock, should be horsewhipped. What would be most fitting is to throw you into a jail cell and deprive you of food and water just as you've done to this poor beast."

Mr. Babcock's eyes narrowed dangerously.

"You got no call to talk to me like that. You git off my property."

"I'll do that," Aunt Nell said. "And I'll get the sheriff up here to arrest you for negligence and abuse."

"Sheriff ain't gonna put me in jail over some worthless horse," Mr. Babcock said.

"There are new laws that address the proper care of animals, and you are in violation of them," Aunt Nell said. I didn't understand half of what Aunt Nell was saying, and I didn't find out till later that Aunt Nell was bluffing, but Mr. Babcock didn't know that.

"Now see here," he said. "I haven't had the money to feed him."

"Looks to me you've had plenty to put in your own belly," Aunt Nell said. She stabbed her finger into his huge stomach, which seemed to me something akin to poking a tiger in a cage. I was afraid Mr. Babcock was going to haul off and punch Aunt Nell, but he just backed away, looking like he wanted to strangle her.

"What'll you give me for him?" Mr. Babcock asked. That showed how much nerve Mr. Babcock had, trying to sell a horse he'd very nearly killed.

"I thought you said he was worthless," Aunt Nell said.

"Leon'll pay me thirty dollars."

Thirty dollars was a princely sum in this, the height of the Depression. I knew Papa didn't have ten dollars to spare to save an old broken-down horse.

"I'll give you forty dollars for him," Aunt Nell said. Again, I stared at her in astonishment. Aunt Nell was full of surprises. But foolish, too. All she had to do was outbid Leon; she probably could have gotten the horse for thirty-one dollars. Still, that was a lot to pay for a horse that couldn't earn its own living.

Mr. Babcock's eyes gleamed greedily.

"It's your money," he said. "Let's see it." He held out his hand.

"I'll pay you when we come to get him in a few days," Aunt Nell said. "I suggest you get him some hay and some water. I'll not be paying for a dead horse," and I realized Aunt Nell wasn't as foolish as I'd thought. For forty dollars, Mr. Babcock would be sure to at least feed the horse till we could pick it up.

"Now that that's settled, there's still the matter of how we are going to get home," Aunt Nell said. "You wouldn't happen to have a beast here that you *haven't* abused to the brink of death, would you?"

Mr. Babcock's eyes darkened, but he said nothing. Aunt Nell had him, and he knew it; he would keep his anger in check until he had that forty dollars in hand.

"No?" Aunt Nell said, eyebrows arched. "Funny, this is just the place I'd expect to find a centaur or Chimera."

A look of confusion crossed Mr. Babcock's face, and I had to hide a smile. I knew what Aunt Nell was referring to: centaurs were half man, half horse, and a Chimera was a creature made up of a lion, goat, and serpent who'd been killed by Bellerophon on his winged horse Pegasus (Papa always did say I read too much mythology), but Mr. Babcock was too ignorant to know he was being insulted.

"Only other animal I got is a bull, and he's plenty healthy," Mr. Babcock said. "I hire him out to—" he stopped, flustered, and a red blush crept up his neck.

Growing up on a farm had also taught me where babies come from, and I'd seen our bull service our cows, but as coarse as Mr. Babcock was, even he wouldn't discuss such matters with a woman.

"Well, then, could we borrow your bull?" Aunt Nell asked, as sweet as could be.

Now I looked as confused as Mr. Babcock. What could Aunt Nell possibly want with Mr. Babcock's bull?

When Mr. Babcock didn't answer, Aunt Nell explained.

"I plan to have your bull pull our buggy home," she said.

Aunt Nell might as well have said that she was going to sprout wings and fly to the moon.

"Now you're just funning with me," Mr. Babcock said.

"I'm perfectly serious," Aunt Nell said.

"Then you're plain crazy," Mr. Babcock said. "There's no way you'd ever get that bull hitched up, much less get home without getting killed."

"I'll make a deal with you," Aunt Nell said, her voice chill as a January night. "If I do get the bull hitched up and home, you'll let me borrow your automobile one day next week."

"If you don't take the cake," Mr. Babcock said and grinned confidently. "Lady, if you can get him hitched up, you can *have* my automobile!"

I never could figure out how Aunt Nell did it. She climbed over the fence and started toward him. The bull had his head down, watching her, and he was pawing the ground something fierce. I would have run for the hills but not Aunt Nell. She started talking to him, low. I couldn't make out what she was saying, but the bull's ears twitched like he was listening to her. When she got close enough, she touched his head, still whispering to him, and I wondered if she put some kind of spell on him because, even though he snorted and kicked, he let Aunt Nell lead him out of the pasture and hitch him up to the buggy. You could have stored butternuts in Mr. Babcock's mouth, it was hanging open so.

Keeping a tight hold on the reins, Aunt Nell climbed into the buggy.

"I guess we're about set," she said. "Mr. Babcock, would you care to ride with us?"

Mr. Babcock shook his head slowly.

"I wouldn't set foot in that buggy for a thousand dollars," he said.

I didn't want to set foot in that buggy, either. I was sure Aunt Nell and I were riding to our deaths, but I climbed in, my legs shaking, and sat beside her.

"Bring the car by the Randall's place first thing on Monday morning," Aunt Nell said. "We'll drop you off back here before we get on our way."

At the mention of his car, and realizing that it was no longer his because of his rash promise, Mr.

Babcock's face drained of color. Aunt Nell let him suffer for a few moments while she struggled to control the bull, then she spoke.

"Don't worry, Mr. Babcock, I'm only going to borrow your automobile for Monday. But next time, maybe you'll take care not to underestimate the capabilities of a woman."

Mr. Babcock, relief flooding his face ruddy again, nodded meekly. And with that, Aunt Nell let the bull run. I didn't have time to ask why she needed his car.

I grabbed the dashboard and held on for all I was worth. We careened down hills and around corners, narrowly missing trees and rocks. A few times I felt all four wheels leave the ground. I prayed we wouldn't meet anyone; it'd be a shame to cause someone else's death besides our own.

Aunt Nell seemed to be having the time of her life. She had her feet braced, and the muscles in her arms bulged as she pulled with all her strength, but I couldn't see that she was slowing that bull down one iota. Her hair had come loose from its bun, and I imagined her as one of those larger-than-life Greek or Roman goddesses. She could be Europa, who'd tamed a white bull and ridden him to the island of Crete. The only trouble was that Mr. Babcock's bull wasn't white, and most of those mythological heroes ended up dead.

"Aunt Nell, is he running away?" I shouted.

"Why, I suppose he is," Aunt Nell said as we bounced over ruts. "At least he's running in the right direction. We'll be home in no time flat."

If we lived, I thought.

We careened into the yard on two wheels. Grandma, Mama, and Emily heard the commotion and tumbled onto the porch. They all stared, mouths open, at the sight of us.

"Good gracious!" Grandma said when she'd found her voice. "I've never seen the like. Sister, I hope you haven't had trouble."

Aunt Nell looked at me, and we both laughed. I felt giddy with relief, so certain had I been that we would be killed. I was even glad to see Emily.

"Why, no, sister," Aunt Nell said. "We haven't had a bit of trouble. We've seen a little of the countryside, and I have managed to borrow a car to take the girls to the circus. Other than that, it's been an uneventful morning."

And that is how I came to own a horse.

6

For some reason, Aunt Nell didn't mention Mr. Babcock's horse when she was relating the story of how she came to drive a bull home. Perhaps she was embarrassed, certain that Papa, Mama, and Grandma, too, would think her foolish to waste so much money on such a sorry creature. So I didn't tell, either, though I was bursting to. Mr. Babcock's horse was no Black Beauty. And he was so broken down, I doubted I'd ever be able to ride him. Still, Aunt Nell had saved him from the slaughter yard, and I was glad. Now I'd have to make a place for him when he arrived.

I spent the afternoon in the barn, cleaning out

the extra horse stall. Papa had stored equipment, tools, and sacks of feed in there, and it took me the better part of three hours to clear all that stuff out. I was hot and dirty by the time I'd moved and stacked everything and was dreaming of that cold water in the quarry when Emily waltzed in.

"Whatcha doing?" she asked.

I was caught unawares. The horse was a secret, and I hadn't thought of how I would explain my sudden burst of tidiness.

"Just cleaning," I said, my mind searching for a lie that would satisfy Emily.

"Why?"

"I wanted to do something nice for Papa," I said and wanted to kick myself as soon as I said it. What was wrong with me? I could lie better than that.

Emily eyed me suspiciously. She knew better than to believe I'd be doing such a job out of the goodness of my heart.

"You'd better tell me what's going on," Emily

said, "or I'll tell Papa I found you out here, up to no good."

I almost laughed. I mean, what was she going to tell Papa, anyway—that I was cleaning out a stall? Hardly something that would call for punishment. But Papa would wonder why I was doing it, and there'd be questions, and I'd have to invent a story that would convince him. I figured I'd take my chances with Emily.

"Promise you won't tell?" I said, which was like asking a person with hay fever not to sneeze. Emily nodded.

"Making a place for my horse," I told her, proudly, and went on to describe Aunt Nell's encounter with Mr. Babcock.

Emily was unimpressed.

"Mama won't let you keep it," she said, all high-and-mighty.

I'd worried about that, too, but I wasn't going to give Emily the satisfaction of thinking she was right.

"You got to keep the kitten, didn't you? And

Aunt Nell's buying the horse, so she gets to say what happens to it. And she said she bought it for me, so there."

"She won't let you keep it," Emily repeated, infuriatingly.

I glared at her, thinking again how much I hated her and wanted to slap that smug face of hers. Mama probably wouldn't let me keep the horse. Emily always got whatever she wanted, and she delighted in rubbing my nose in the fact that everyone loved her more than they did me. I'd find a way to get back at her, even if it took all night to think it up.

I chose the next morning for my revenge since I knew Mama, Grandma, and Aunt Nell were going visiting.

I watched from the barn until they left, went over the plan again quickly in my head, and took a deep breath. I'd have to be convincing.

Emily was sweeping when I burst through the door.

"Help! Help!" I called, wringing my hands. "Oh, Emily, hurry! Whiskers is drowning!"

The broom clattered to the floor.

"Drowning?" Emily cried. "Where?"

"In the quarry," I said. "Hurry. You're the only one who can save him."

Emily was too upset to question why she alone could rescue the cat. She ran across the fields, moaning, "Whiskers, oh, my poor Whiskers," every few feet, with me in hot pursuit, urging her to hurry. I didn't want her to have time to think about the snakes and turn back. I was feeling pretty pleased with my performance, too. Maybe I would pursue acting when I grew up, be a film star like Lillian Gish or Clara Bow.

Emily reached the quarry's edge, and her eyes scanned the water's surface.

"Whiskers! Whiskers!" she called. "Oh, Lily, where was he?"

"Right there!" I hollered gleefully and shoved her off the edge.

If she'd just let herself fall, Emily would have been all right. It was only about ten feet down to the water, and she would have bobbed back to the surface and swum to shore, mad as a wet cat, no doubt, but unharmed. But instead, she twisted in midair, scrambling to catch hold of the rocks, and in doing so, her head hit against the rocks as she fell. When I peered over the edge, she was floating face down in the water, not moving.

Panic gripped my heart. Had I killed her?

"Emily!" I screamed and jumped in beside her.

I got hold of her collar and dragged her to shore. I hauled her up on the rocks, rolling her face up, and stared at her pale face. There was blood on her temple, and I wondered how I could ever go home and tell Mama and Papa that I'd killed Emily. I'd have to run away, live out the rest of my days as a fugitive.

"Emily!" I yelled again and shook her. "Emily!"

Emily groaned, and I went limp with relief. She wasn't dead after all.

Her eyes fluttered open.

"You're all right," I told her. "You hit your head."

She put her hand up to her forehead, winced as she touched the bruise, and looked at her hand.

"I'm bleeding!"

"Oh, don't be such a baby. It's just a tiny cut," I said, though the lump on her head had swollen to near egg size. "If you'd just fallen like you were supposed to, you wouldn't have gotten hurt."

"I'm telling Mama," she sniffed. "And then you won't be able to go to the circus."

What she said was true, and I had to think fast.

"If you tell, then I'll have to tell Mama that you got knocked out, and Mama will make you rest, and you won't be able to go either."

Emily must have figured I was right because when Mama, Grandma, and Aunt Nell arrived home, she'd arranged her hair to cover the cut and never breathed a word that I'd near killed her.

Later, when we were in bed, I heard Emily sniffling.

"What's the matter?" I asked.

"My head hurts," Emily said.

Here she goes, I thought. I'm never going to hear the end of it, how I tricked her and hurt her. But Emily surprised me.

"I guess I deserved it," Emily said. "I'm sorry I was so mean about the horse."

As near as I could recollect, Emily had never apologized to me. Before I even knew I'd opened my mouth, I heard myself saying, "I'm sorry I pushed you into the quarry," and as soon as I said it, I *was* sorry that I'd pushed her. That's what's funny about talking in the dark. You can say things that you never would face-to-face.

"When you get your horse, will you let me ride it?" Emily asked.

"I don't think Mama's going to let either of us ride it," I answered.

There was silence.

"She wouldn't see us if we practiced up by the quarry," Emily said, and I grinned in the dark. I actually *liked* Emily, when she wasn't being bossy or a Miss Goody Two-Shoes. Which is almost never.

"I thought you were scared to go up there," I said.

"I am, a little," Emily said. "But I want to be braver. More like you," and then I was so dumbstruck that by the time I'd thought of something to say, Emily was asleep.

7

It was still dark when I poked Emily.

"Get up," I said as I leaped from bed and dressed. When Emily didn't move, I poked her again.

"It's too early," she moaned.

"As soon as we get our work done, we can leave for the circus. Come on."

Emily pulled the sheet over her head.

"I don't feel well," she whined. Whining is something else Emily does when Mama is not around, but after last night, I hadn't expected it. I wondered if I'd dreamed our little talk. Emily had been so nice, but now she was back to her old self.

Any other day I would have flown at her in a rage, but I dared not do anything that might cause Mama to say we couldn't go. Still, I bubbled inside. Oh, Emily wasn't fooling me; she'd pulled this before as an excuse to get out of her share of the work. As soon as I finished all the morning chores, she'd get up and announce she felt better. I'd fix her.

I swept half of the floors, set half of the table, gathered exactly half of the eggs. When Emily did get up, she'd have to hustle to finish her work, or she'd get left behind. And she'd get scolded, for a change, instead of me.

Mama was stirring up a batch of graham rolls when I came in from the barn and set the basket on the table.

"Is that all the eggs?" she asked.

"No, Mama. I left the other half for Emily to get."

"Where is Emily?" Mama asked, as she spooned the batter into the heavy cast-iron pans and set them in the oven. "Isn't she up yet?"

I shook my head.

"She wouldn't get up," I said. "She *said* she was sick." I put special emphasis on "said" so Mama would know I didn't believe it. Mama hated tattling, but I figured I was only answering her questions. I couldn't be accused of tattling doing that, could I?

"Really?" Mama said, wiping her hands on her apron. "I'll go check on her while you gather the rest of those eggs. And set the rest of the table, too, while you're at it. Goodness, Lily, where's your head this morning?"

I was so hot with injustice, I broke two of the eggs and had to drop them in the gutter so Mama wouldn't see. She counted on her egg money and wouldn't take kindly to me breaking some out of carelessness. I wanted to crack them over Emily's head. Sick indeed. Emily could fool Mama but not me. And I just burned at how Mama catered to her every whim. If I'd said I was sick, Mama would have told me to stop lollygagging and finish my chores.

Aunt Nell and Grandma were in the kitchen, serving up the rolls and oatmeal when I came in.

I loved graham rolls, and I even liked oatmeal, but I was too wound up to eat.

"I'm not hungry, Grandma," I said.

"You're not leaving until you eat," Grandma said, so I gobbled my breakfast and waited impatiently for Aunt Nell to finish hers. We heard Mr. Babcock's automobile pull up into the yard.

"Time to go," I said, grabbing the basket lunch that Mama had made up for us the night before.

"Where's Emily?" Aunt Nell asked. "Is she ready?"

"Emily might not be able to go," I said hopefully. "She said she was sick."

"Oh, dear," Grandma said, and we heard Mama's footsteps on the stairs.

"Is Emily coming with us to the circus, Maggie?" Aunt Nell asked Mama.

"I'm afraid not," Mama said. "She says her head hurts and her legs ache. She does feel feverish."

"You and Edna have a lot to do today," Aunt Nell said. "I could stay with her."

My jaw dropped. Aunt Nell would ruin our day together just to stay with Emily? Why did she come first with everybody?

"Nonsense," Mama said. "I'm going to make her some tea, and I'll dose her with some castor oil. I'm sure she'll be fine."

At mention of the castor oil, I grinned. That'd teach Emily to fake being sick. Castor oil was awful, and it stuck in your throat for hours.

Aunt Nell picked up her purse and nodded to me.

"I guess it's just you and me," Aunt Nell said, and her words were music to my ears. Just Aunt Nell and me and no Emily. Perfect.

Mr. Babcock had shaved, put on a clean shirt and, as we drove back to his place to drop him off, he acted almost friendly, but I couldn't forgive him for how he'd treated his horse. He showed Aunt Nell how to shift gears, brake and accelerate, signal turns, and what to do should it begin to rain. He even told her to park the car behind the horse barns so it wouldn't get scratched.

It was a relief to leave him off at his place. Aunt Nell told him we'd return the car in the morning, when we came to pick up the horse.

"I couldn't wait to get rid of him," Aunt Nell said. "Goodness, he acted as if I didn't know a thing. And what a slowpoke! We'll get this car moving!" She pressed the accelerator to the floor, and I gripped the door handle tightly, expecting a hair-raising ride, but the car wouldn't respond. It chugged up the hills sluggishly, and it was only after we'd cleared the heights near Sheffield and it was downhill all the way to Lyndonville that the car really got rolling.

It was the first time I'd ridden in an automobile. More and more families in our area had gotten cars, but Papa said he'd stick with horses. They were more reliable, worked in any kind of weather, and didn't have a motor. Papa didn't trust anything that couldn't be stopped by shouting "whoa."

As exciting as it was, I guessed I'd stick with horses myself, and I had to admit that riding in an automobile wasn't half as thrilling as the ride with Aunt Nell and the bull had been. I wondered if the circus might be interested in a bull that could pull a buggy, but Mr. Babcock had sold him, too. Giles Perron, the cattle dealer, had come by our farm to pick him up.

Lyndonville was the biggest town I'd ever seen—a confusion of cars and trucks, people bustling about talking and shouting, dogs barking; all of it both wonderful and fearful to behold. I stuck to Aunt Nell like glue, afraid I'd get separated from her and afraid I'd miss something. When I wondered aloud if New York City or Chicago could seem any grander than Lyndonville, Aunt Nell smiled and said they were both a mite bigger.

Aunt Nell treated me to cotton candy and a candied apple and bought peanuts for me to feed the elephants. I'd expected wild, trumpeting beasts like I'd read about, but these elephants only shuffled from side to side, occasionally flinging dust over their backs. They didn't seem exciting or dangerous, just bored and resigned, and I was horrified to see how the chains had worn sores on their legs. Suddenly, I wanted to go home, and when Aunt Nell asked if I wanted to see the animals in their cages, the tigers and lions and monkeys, I shook my head no, too full of pity for them to speak.

"Good," Aunt Nell said. "Neither do I. I never could bear to see a wild animal caged." Aunt Nell and I seemed to agree on everything.

The show was about to begin, and as we settled into our seats, I had my revelation. Instead of being a missionary like Aunt Nell, I could join the circus and care for the animals. If I couldn't free them, at least I would make sure they were all treated kindly. I would become a performer, too, with my picture on posters, and people would travel from far and wide to see me.

When the woman walked across the high-wire, I saw myself balancing the long pole and feeling for the wire with my toes. I watched the acrobats carefully so that I could practice those tumbles and spins up in the hayloft, and when the trapeze artist flew through the air, I said to myself, *There, that is my future,* but I had not seen my destiny until the announcer pointed our attention to a forty-foot steel tower looming in front of the grandstand. I'd wondered what it was for.

"Ladies and Gentlemen!" the announcer boomed. "You are about to Witness the Most Amazing, the Most Spellbinding, Death-Defying Act Ever Performed—the Diving Horse! From that Tower, the Lovely Marlene and her horse, King, will leap Forty Feet into the Water Tank Below! Forty Feet, Ladies and Gentlemen!"

The crowd cheered.

My breath caught in my throat. A horse was going to jump from there? The tower was taller than our barn. I tried to imagine jumping from the barn roof and could not.

The voice of a man behind us broke into my thoughts.

"There used to be two horses with this outfit, King and Queen," the man told the boy sitting next to him. "But a couple of months ago, when they were someplace in New York, something happened to the front ramp and made Queen jump crooked. She hit the edge of the tank on the way down. Was killed instantly."

I heard not a peep from the boy, and I imagined him to be as stunned as I was. I studied the tower in alarm, looking for weaknesses.

"Guess they'll be looking for another horse to replace her," the man said.

A long ramp at the rear of the tower allowed the horse to climb to the top, and a short ramp at the front overlooked the water tank. I prayed nothing would happen to the front ramp today.

We sat hushed as the lovely Marlene called to King, and he began to climb the ramp slowly. He stopped halfway and had to be called again. I wondered if he'd seen Queen leap to her death.

At the top, Marlene swung onto him, bareback, smiling and waving to the crowd, and urged King down the front ramp until he stood at the edge, but he was leaning back so far his haunches were resting on the ramp, almost as if he were sitting. I felt sorry for him, he seemed so reluctant. That water tank had to seem a long way down. I wondered what it would be like to be on him, looking down, preparing to jump, and my stomach flip-flopped with a curious mixture of dread and anticipation.

They stood poised on that tower, and the crowd sat breathless and waiting. I could see Marlene talking to King, and without warning, he leaped.

They were a blur, horse and rider merged into one like some ancient mythological beast or two celestial beings hurtled to earth by angry gods.

I hadn't wanted to watch, had not wanted King to jump, but when he leaped, something within me leaped, too. For a moment, it was as if I defied gravity. I felt suspended in air, like I had sprouted wings, then I was falling through space with the rush of wind in my ears.

Just above the tank, with only a second to spare, Marlene hurled herself free, and I saw two splashes—one large and one small—as they hit the water. Seconds later, two heads rose, swimming side by side to the tank's edge.

I did not hear the roar of the crowd as they rose around me, clapping and screaming, or see

Marlene and King emerge, dripping and triumphant, for I now knew my heart's desire. Someday, I would be that girl on the diving horse, riding my own Pegasus from the heavens.

"You're awfully quiet," Aunt Nell said as we rode home. "Did you have a good time?"

"Oh, yes," I breathed, "especially the diving horse." But I said no more about it. I was not ready to share my heart's desire just yet, not even with Aunt Nell.

"I didn't really see the horse dive," Aunt Nell admitted. "I was so nervous, I had my eyes closed until I heard the splash. That girl takes a terrible risk." This from a woman who'd driven a bull in a buggy.

Aunt Nell shook her head.

"Can you imagine doing anything so foolhardy?" she asked.

I leaned back and closed my eyes. Yes, I could.

Just as a horse always trots faster when it's headed home, the car no longer seemed sluggish, and we charged up the heights, the miles rolling away behind us. Lulled by the sound of the wheels on the road and the warm golden light, I was half asleep by the time Aunt Nell pulled into our driveway and shut off the motor.

"Someone's visiting," Aunt Nell said, and I struggled to a sitting position to peer through the windshield.

"That's Dr. Pembroke's car," I said. Aunt Nell and I looked at each other. Doctor's visits were expensive. Mama and Grandma knew enough to handle most ailments and injuries we incurred. If Dr. Pembroke had been called, it had to be something serious.

We found Papa at the table, his head in his hands.

"Wesley, what's happened?" Aunt Nell asked.

Papa lifted his head, and the anguish in his eyes stilled my heart.

"Emily has polio," he said.

8

*P*olio. The very word filled parents' hearts with terror. Every year we heard of one or two folks who caught it, but the last local outbreak of any size had been back in 1914. It had killed five people and left nine others in braces and wheel-chairs, but that had been a long time ago, and none of us kids worried about it too much.

Dr. Pembroke told Mama and Papa that Emily's only hope was a new machine that a friend of his from medical school had invented. It was known as the Drinker apparatus, but some folks had started calling it the iron lung. He said the polio had affected the muscles that made it possible for Emily to breathe, and she would suffocate without it. Normally, he would take a patient in Emily's condition to the hospital, but he felt Emily would not survive the trip, so he was going to try to arrange for an iron lung to be sent from the university hospital on the train. He went on to say that some people get well enough that they can leave the iron lung and live without it, but he didn't want to give us any false hope. He said Emily's condition was very grave, and he did not think she would be one of those people.

I heard all this as I was eavesdropping outside the door to our room. I wasn't allowed to see Emily (Mama was afraid I would catch it, too), but I trembled each time I heard her cry out. The disease made her skin and muscles so sensitive to the slightest touch that she couldn't bear the pressure of a nightgown or a sheet upon her. Even the gentlest breeze on her skin caused agony, so the windows were closed and the house seemed as hot and airless as an oven.

Dr. Pembroke's words hit me like a sledgehammer. I had no idea what an iron lung was or what it looked like, but it sounded horrible. I hadn't thought before that Emily would do anything other than get well and be the way she'd always been, and I stood stunned against the wall. No one knew for sure how people got polio, but every summer we were warned against swimming in public places, and the town closed down the beach at the lake. I'd pushed Emily into the quarry, and she had gotten polio. Maybe it was my fault Emily was sick. My fault she had to be in an iron lung. She might even die, and that would be my fault, too.

I closed my eyes as waves of nausea washed over me. Oh, if only I could go back a day, a week, I would change everything. I wouldn't be selfish or mean. I would be a good sister to Emily. Dear God, I prayed, let her get well, and I'll never be angry at her again.

Papa and Mama must have realized more than I that Emily might die or end up crippled, but they seemed stunned, too, by Dr. Pembroke's words. There was a moment of silence before Papa spoke.

"An iron lung machine?" he said.

"Yes."

"Is it run by electricity?" Papa asked.

"Yes."

"But we don't have electricity," Papa said.

"I'm going to see what we can do about that, too," Dr. Pembroke said. "How close is the nearest pole?"

Silence again while Papa thought.

"Over at Bert Wallace's. That's about three-quarters of a mile."

"I'll go right to the utility when I get back to town," Dr. Pembroke said. "Your daughter's life depends on this."

"An iron lung," I heard Mama say after Dr. Pembroke had gone. (I'd ducked into the hall closet when he left so he wouldn't know I'd been eavesdropping.) I heard fear in Mama's voice. "It must be terribly expensive. And getting electricity put in. How will we pay for all that?"

More silence.

"I don't know," Papa said in a voice so flat and empty I didn't recognize it as his. "You know we don't have two nickels to rub together, and ever since the storm, the bank has practically owned the farm. But what choice do we have?"

The storm Papa was referring to had happened three years before. Lightning had killed all twelve of our cows one night as they huddled under a tree. Papa had borrowed heavily to replace them, and he hadn't been able to pay that back.

By midafternoon, a crew of men and trucks from the utility appeared. Papa worked alongside them, digging holes, setting poles, and stringing wire. Aunt Nell and Grandma furnished them all with sandwiches and hot coffee to keep them going. The men worked through the night, and by morning we had electricity in our house. It was downstairs only, but it seemed like magic to flip a switch and have a room light up. Now, someday, we could get an electric stove instead of the hot, black cookstove and a refrigerator instead of the messy icebox. I knew I also wouldn't miss having to clean the sooty chimneys of the kerosene lamps.

Papa invited the men to stay for breakfast.

There were tears in his eyes when he thanked each man.

"I'd string line every night for pancakes like this," one man said jokingly to Grandma, then remembered what he'd been stringing the line for. He ducked his head in embarrassment.

"We just hope your girl gets better," he said, and the rest of the men nodded.

After they'd gone, Papa hitched up Bob and Joe to the wagon and drove to the train station to pick up the iron lung.

Dr. Pembroke followed Papa home, bringing a nurse with him who would care for Emily and train Mama, Grandma, and Aunt Nell how to care for her, too. He also brought three men from town to help carry the iron lung into the house.

I'd wondered what an iron lung looked like, but once I saw it, I shuddered at the thought of being entombed in one. It looked like a piece of smooth culvert pipe, a long cylinder of shiny metal, but all I could think of was, it's a prison. A little metal prison. Even the animals at the circus had larger cages to live in.

The iron lung was placed in the living room (it was too heavy to carry upstairs) and plugged in. Emily was carried downstairs and put into it. Only her head stuck out. Along the sides of the iron lung there were portholes that allowed the nurse to care for the patient.

"How's it work?" I asked.

"I don't know," Papa said wearily. I'd never seen him look so stooped. There were dark circles under his eyes, and I realized he hadn't gotten any sleep in the last two days. Neither had Mama, who'd sat vigil by Emily's bed, willing her to live.

Dr. Pembroke explained to all of us how the iron lung worked. Or tried to explain. It had something to do with changing air pressure that would force air in and out of Emily's lungs, but I didn't understand. I don't know if Mama or Papa did, either. The only thing that mattered to us was that once she was in the machine, Emily breathed easier, and that meant we did too.

9

Twenty-four hours a day, the motor on the iron lung pumped with a steady, hissing sound. Dr. Pembroke said we'd get used to the sound, that we wouldn't even notice it after awhile, but he was wrong. The iron lung was like a monster that had taken over the house, filling the living room, and we could hear it breathing. The hissing sound, as steady as a heartbeat or a clock, followed us everywhere. It was there when we woke up and when we slept, when we worked and when we ate. It became a presence in the house, filling my head and my ears until I couldn't remember what life had been like before the sound.

Emily was able to speak only when the iron lung allowed her to. She often had to pause in midsentence while the machine took a breath for her, so she talked in a slow, halting rhythm.

"Are the wild rasp . . . berries ripe?" she'd say, or "Did you feed . . . Whiskers yet?"

Ever since Emily had gotten sick, Whiskers had been forgotten. He moved through the house like a ghost, hiding under beds and chairs. Occasionally, Emily caught sight of him out of the corner of her eye.

"Whiskers," Emily whispered. "Whiskers, come here."

But Whiskers wouldn't go near her. Once, when I carried him over to Emily, he screeched and clawed his way out of my arms, leaving long, bloody furrows. He was scared of the iron lung. I didn't blame him. It scared me, too. I hurried through my household chores as fast as I could, just so I could go outside and escape that hateful sound. Sometimes it seemed as if the iron lung was sucking all the oxygen from the house, and I would stand on the porch gasping for air.

I scared Aunt Nell when she found me there.

"Lily, are you all right?" she asked, anxiously.

I drew in a long, quavering breath.

"Yes. It's just that, well, I have to get out of there sometimes."

Aunt Nell nodded.

"I know what you mean," she said. "I can't bear to see her in that machine. I saw hundreds of polio cases in India, but I never got used to it. Of course, we didn't have anything like iron lungs over there, so cases that were as bad as Emily's always died. But to see all those twisted, crippled people, especially the children, was heartbreaking. And now to have it be my own grandniece. Why couldn't I have been stricken instead of her? I'm an old woman. I've lived my life. Emily is just beginning hers. Such a waste."

I'd been wanting to ask Aunt Nell something, and I jumped in, eager to change the subject.

"Aunt Nell, when can we go get Mr. Babcock's horse?"

Aunt Nell's hand flew to her mouth.

"Oh, my," she said. "I'd completely forgotten

about that. I'll certainly have to contact him and let him know our plans have changed."

"You mean we'll have to wait to get the horse?"

Aunt Nell looked troubled.

"Lily, I'm afraid I won't be able to buy Mr. Babcock's horse after all."

My heart sank to my socks.

"Why not?"

"Well, your father and mother have so many debts, and now with Emily's illness, I know it's weighing heavily on them how they're ever going to pay them. The little bit I've saved isn't going to erase those debts, but they're welcome to everything I have."

"Couldn't you give them everything except the forty dollars?" I knew I was being selfish and hateful, but I couldn't help it. I'd had my heart set on that horse, even if he wasn't Black Beauty.

"No, Lily, I couldn't. Every little bit will help." Her voice softened.

"Emily's going to need so much. Even if she does get out of that machine, she'll be crippled. There'll be therapy and braces and more doctor bills. From now on, I'm afraid everything will have to be about Emily."

"Everything's always been about Emily," I said, softly, and regretted the words as soon as I said them. I mean, I'd meant them, but I hadn't meant to show Aunt Nell how mean and selfish I was.

I expected her to scold me, but she just gave me a strange, sorrowful look.

"You know, I'd do the same if it was you," she said quietly, and I felt even worse.

As I passed by the living room, I heard Grandma singing, and I leaned against the doorframe to listen. Grandma had a washbasin and was washing Emily's hair. Mama had cut Emily's long blond hair short to make it easier to care for. Emily looked so frail, just her little shorn head sticking out of the iron lung. She caught sight of me out of the corner of her eye. She tried to smile, but her face had more the look of a trapped animal.

All afternoon, I considered what I would do. Without Aunt Nell's forty dollars, Mr. Babcock would sell his horse to Leon Benoit, if he hadn't already. If I did nothing, the horse would die, and that was unacceptable. I could buy the horse myself, but I didn't have forty cents much less forty dollars. Even if I could find work with someone in the area (a highly unlikely situation since there were grown men begging for work to feed their families), it would still take me months to earn that much, and I doubted Mr. Babcock would wait that long for his money when he could get thirty dollars from Leon right off. No matter how many ways I played it out in my mind, I still came down to one conclusion: I would have to steal the horse.

Once I'd accepted that in my mind, I sat down to figure out how I would do it and where I would hide him. Obviously, I wouldn't be able to keep him in that stall I'd cleaned out. I tried to think of any old barns or sheds in the area, but nothing sprang to mind. It would have to be someplace where he wouldn't be seen and yet be near feed and water. It was the thought of water that clinched it. The old quarry. No one would see him up there. He'd have grass and water, and I could sneak oats up to him and check on him every day.

Now for getting him. Mr. Babcock lived eight miles away. I'd have to walk there and back, which was sure to take most of a day. Even with everyone focused on Emily, they were sure to notice me gone for a whole day. And how would I explain my absence?

I would have to do it at night.

Once I've set my mind to something, I like to just go ahead and do it. I took a deep breath and decided I would go that very night.

I would be breaking the law. I could go to jail. At the very least, I'd be in a whole lot of trouble. So why was I trembling so with excitement?

I wondered if Bonnie and Clyde had started out this way.

10

Even once my eyes had accustomed themselves to the dark, it was still blacker than the inside of an oven out on that road. I hadn't thought whether there'd be moonlight to see by. There were a lot of things I hadn't planned out well. I'd been so concerned with sneaking out quietly, I hadn't thought to bring along something to eat or drink. I was so thirsty at one point, I scooped up water from a small brook beside the road and drank it. I hoped it was clean water. That'd be just my luck to die from typhus or cholera. Maybe it'd be God's way of punishing me for stealing. Or for what I'd done to Emily.

I plodded along, feeling the road with my feet, and jumped at every sound. I imagined all sorts of predators lurking about, ready to grab me. Mama always said I had too vivid an imagination.

After a few miles, my shoe began to wear a blister on my right foot. At first it was only a mild distraction, but then it began to burn like fire. With each painful step, my enthusiasm faded. It seemed like I'd already walked twenty miles, and yet I still was not to Mr. Babcock's.

I recited poems in my head: *The wind was a torrent of darkness among the gusty trees, the moon was a ghostly galleon tossed upon cloudy seas.* I listed the kings and queens of England, in order, and I tried to remember the capitals of all the African countries. I passed the old dance hall where Papa had first set eyes on Mama and, had it been light, I could've seen Mr. Babcock's place just ahead. I felt my heart racing and was glad it was such a dark night. It would be harder to find my way behind the barn and get the horse, but it would also be harder for someone to see me. Someone being Mr. Babcock.

A dog barked. I jumped, and my blood congealed in my veins. I hadn't seen a dog at Mr. Babcock's before. I wondered how it would feel when the dog's teeth tore into my flesh.

"Shut up," I heard Mr. Babcock growl, and the dog quieted.

At his voice, I ducked quickly and crouched under the bushes along the road.

I heard men's voices and wondered if they could hear my heart thudding against my ribs. It sounded as loud as a drum to me. My nerve evaporated in the night air. Why had I considered doing such a foolish thing? I'd expected Mr. Babcock to be asleep. I hadn't counted on him being up and outside at this time of night. And who were these other men? What was going on?

Trying to forget that curiosity killed the cat, I crawled closer to see if I could determine what Mr. Babcock was up to.

There were three of them in all, and they were carrying boxes from the shed and loading them into Mr. Babcock's car, but I couldn't figure out what they were doing until one of the men stumbled and cursed. I heard the clink of bottles.

"Watch your step, you idiot," the other man hissed. "You break those bottles and the boss'll have us killed. This whiskey's worth more than you and me put together."

Whiskey! They were smuggling whiskey!

Prohibition, the law that made it illegal to buy or sell liquor, had been in effect for twelve years, but even Papa, who didn't drink, thought it was a bad law.

"It's created a crime wave in this country," I'd heard him say many times. "Those that want liquor are getting it anyway, and it's just made a lot of crooks rich. Some of them are willing to kill just to get rich." It seemed true what Papa said. We'd all read stories in the newspapers of gangland killings.

Remembering his words, I realized for the first time what danger I was in. What if Mr. Babcock caught me? He could kill me. He could bury me somewhere out here, and no one would ever be the wiser. My family would never know what had happened to me.

Images flashed through my mind of being buried alive, dirt filling my mouth and ears and eyes, clawing with my fingers. . . . I shuddered. My imagination at work again.

With trembling hands, I felt my way along the barn wall. I would have to be extra careful not to be seen, but at least Mr. Babcock was distracted.

I ran right into the horse and scared us both. The horse snorted, and I expected Mr. Babcock to come tearing around the corner of the barn, shotgun blazing, but nothing happened. I felt my way to the horse's head, and my heart sank when I realized I'd forgotten to bring a halter. Stupid me. I hadn't even thought to bring a rope. Where was my head? Well, if Aunt Nell could hitch a bull to a buggy, surely I could figure out a way to lead a sick horse home.

All I can say is that I was doubly glad for the darkness that night. I wouldn't have wanted anyone to see me as I led the horse home with my coveralls wrapped around his neck. I've heard of a horselaugh, and I could have sworn I heard this horse chuckle at the sight of my pale, bare legs, but perhaps it was only my acute embarrassment that made me think so, for the horse was suffering his own misery that night, being in no condition to walk eight miles. I wondered if I could even get him home and had to tug on him often to keep him moving.

I don't know when I'd been so happy to see my home. I went past the buildings and led the horse up to the quarry. I didn't tie him. If he wanted, he could have hightailed it, but I didn't think he would; his legs were trembling so, I was afraid he'd fall. I piled oats and corn and fresh green grass in front of him, patted him goodnight, and went to the house, sneaking in the back way so as not to wake up anyone in the family or the nurse who slept on a cot next to Emily.

My bed had never felt so good, and I sank gratefully into blessed sleep. Before I closed my eyes, I offered one little prayer. If God was still listening to me, I promised not to make a career as a thief.

11

Someone grabbed me from behind. I tried to scream, but the man put a gag in my mouth and tied my hands behind my back. Though I struggled to escape, he was strong and shoved me into the backseat of his car. As he climbed behind the steering wheel, I saw that it was Mr. Babcock. He turned and grinned at me.

"They'll wonder what happened to you," he said, and I understood that he intended to kill me. He was taking me where I would not be found.

"Lily."

I struggled to get my hands free. Mama. Papa. Help. Save me.

"Lily." I felt a cool hand on my forehead and jerked my head away.

"Lily, wake up."

I opened my eyes. Mama was bending over me, her eyes registering alarm.

"You don't feel feverish," she said. "Are you sick?"

I wondered at her question. Why would she think I was sick? Had I called out during my nightmare?

"No, Mama. I'm all right."

"I couldn't wake you," Mama said. "It's past ten o'clock."

Ten o'clock! I'd never slept so late. But then, I'd never stayed up all night either.

"Are you sure you're all right?" Mama asked. "You're not achy or anything?"

"No, Mama. I'm just tired."

Mama's shoulders sagged with relief.

"Thank the Lord," she said. "Tired I can understand. I've never been so exhausted." She rubbed her neck. She'd never looked so exhausted, either. Dark circles under her eyes made her look like a raccoon, a tired raccoon, and she'd lost enough weight that the bones in her face stood out. Still, it wasn't like Mama to complain.

"Well, get dressed, then," Mama said. "Grandma's kept some breakfast warm for you." She hesitated.

"One more thing, Lily," Mama added. "I want you to spend more time with Emily. Lying in that iron lung, with nothing to do, makes for very long days. You could make them go by faster by talking more to her."

"I don't know what to say to her," I fairly screeched. "What will I talk about?"

"Goodness, Lily," Mama said, wearily. "There's no reason to work yourself up into a lather. Tell her stories or jokes. Read to her."

So, each evening, after chores and supper, no matter how tired I was, I read to Emily: *Little Women* (I tried skipping the part where Beth dies, but Emily wouldn't let me), *My Antonia, The*

Wind in the Willows. She especially liked *My Antonia.*

"I can almost feel . . . that prairie wind," she said. "Imagine a place . . . with no trees . . . or mountains."

"We'll go to the prairie, someday," I said, and could have bitten my tongue. "You know, when you get out of that ir . . . when you get better." I was stammering now. "You'll go to lots of places."

Emily's lips trembled.

"When you read . . ." she said, "I go to those pla . . . ces in my mind."

Her words filled me with shame. I thought of all the times I'd fled to the barn and the garden and the fields, just so I wouldn't have to listen to the iron lung. Emily couldn't run from it. The only way she could escape was by imagining herself in the places I read about.

At least once a day, I managed to sneak away from the house and carry oats and corn to the horse. I wondered how long it would be before Papa noticed the missing grain. I'd have to come up with some explanation, but I'd cross that bridge when I came to it. Right now I was enjoying having a horse. He was always watching for me, and I made sure he was near plenty of tall green grass, and I kept his bucket filled with water. I knew I was taking good care of him. What I didn't know was that I was taking *too* good care of him. He was getting too much to eat.

I'd done up the dishes one morning, swept the floor and picked and shelled two rows of peas. I had a few minutes before Grandma would need my help getting dinner ready. I dashed up to the quarry, carrying a bucket of grain.

I knew as soon as I saw my horse that something was wrong. He stood with his forefeet stuck far out in front of him and his hind legs under him, almost as if he were about to sit down. I called to him, then tugged on him, but he refused to move.

Sick at heart, I ran for home. It was almost noon, and Papa had just come in to wash up for dinner.

"Oh, Papa, hurry," I said. "Please hurry."

My tone of voice must have scared him, for he

ran behind me all the way back to the quarry without saying a word. Papa took in the scene with one glance.

"Lily May Randall," he said, his voice as dark as a thundercloud. "Whose horse is this?"

"Mine," I said, lifting my chin bravely, but the squeak in my voice gave me away.

Papa's eyes shot lightning bolts through me, and I hung my head. Papa didn't tolerate lying.

"Mr. Babcock's," I said.

"What's Duncan Babcock's horse doing here?" Papa asked. "I want the truth, Lily."

"I took him," I whispered.

"What?"

It was time to face the music. I sighed and looked Papa in the face.

"I stole him."

Papa took a step back. He couldn't have looked more stunned if I'd whacked him over the head with the post maul. It was some minutes before he knew what to say, and I spent all of that time wishing I'd never met Mr. Babcock or his horse.

"I can't believe a daughter of mine would do such a thing," Papa said, slowly and sorrowfully. "I didn't raise you up to be a thief."

"No, Papa," I said, miserably. My idea to steal Mr. Babcock's horse, which had made so much sense a few days ago, now seemed like the dumbest idea in history.

"I honestly don't know what to do with you, Lily," Papa said. "I still can't believe you stole a horse."

I hadn't noticed that Aunt Nell had followed, and I jumped when she spoke.

"I'm afraid I'm to blame for this, Wesley," she said. "Mr. Babcock was going to send that horse to slaughter, and I agreed to buy it from him. But after Emily got sick, I told Lily I'd be using all my money to help with Emily's expenses."

"That doesn't excuse her," Papa said, his eyes still smoldering. "Lily's old enough to understand that life doesn't always turn out the way we want it to. And if she doesn't know it by now, then it's time she learned it, for Christ's sake!"

His words set me to trembling. Papa almost

never swore—only when he was mightily provoked.

"First thing we're going to do is ride over to
Mr. Babcock's and pay him his money. And you,
Lily, are going to apologize to him."

"Let me handle this, Wesley," Aunt Nell said.
"I'm at least partially responsible. I'll take Lily
over to Mr. Babcock's and see that things are put
to right."

"What about him?" I asked.

"Who?" Papa said.

"The horse."

"Oh," Papa said. "I'll take care of him until you
get back."

I hated leaving my horse, but I didn't want to
make Papa any angrier by arguing with him, so I
went with Aunt Nell. She hitched Lady to the
buggy, told Grandma we'd be back in time for
supper, and off we went.

I rode in silence for the first few miles, feeling
ashamed and wondering how I could have made
such a mess of things. Aunt Nell was the first to
speak.

"Your papa wouldn't want to hear me say this," she said, "but I think you did the right thing. I never should have backed out of the deal in the first place. It was wrong of me not to hold up my end of the bargain."

Her sympathy was almost harder to bear than a scolding. I sagged against her, my throat hot with tears. Aunt Nell put one arm around me and kissed the top of my head.

"I understand why you did what you did. Had I been in your shoes, I guess I would have done the same thing. Just don't do it again."

I wiped my nose and nodded. I wanted to hug Aunt Nell, but instead, I told her about seeing the whiskey runners at Mr. Babcock's.

"Bootleggers!" Aunt Nell exclaimed. Then her eyes turned dark. "That would explain a lot: how he supports himself, now that he's sold off his cows. And that's why he was almost pleasant when he lent us his car."

"What do you mean?"

"Remember when we were driving to Lyndonville? I thought the car seemed to be riding low.

We were transporting whiskey for that man without even knowing it. I'm sure of it. Mr. Babcock figured two women wouldn't arouse suspicion. And remember how he told me to park the car behind the horse barns? Undoubtedly, he had someone there to unload the car."

She didn't say another word, but her jaw was clenched, and her eyes flashed. I almost felt sorry for Mr. Babcock.

Aunt Nell rapped loudly on his door and tapped her foot impatiently until he opened it.

"Mr. Babcock," Aunt Nell said, coolly. "We meet again."

"What are you doing here?"

"We've come to pay you for your horse."

Mr. Babcock's eyes narrowed.

"That horse ain't here no more. Some no-account stole it."

If I hadn't been so nervous, I would have laughed. Mr. Babcock calling someone else a no-account was like the pot calling the kettle black.

"That's why we've come," Aunt Nell said, "to make things right."

"You took my horse?" Mr. Babcock said, and his eyes gleamed. "You were going to sic the sheriff on me, and now it looks like you'll be going to jail your own self." He almost giggled.

"Aunt Nell didn't steal your horse," I said in a small voice. "I did."

"You?" Mr. Babcock said. "Well, now, won't that be a pretty sight, you and your aunt sharing a jail cell." He shoved his face near mine, and I could smell his rotting teeth.

"Little miss high-and-mighty, thinking you could just waltz in here and steal my horse," he said.

I wondered how I was possibly going to apologize to this man.

"Lily said you had company that night she came here."

"Company?" Mr. Babcock licked his lips nervously.

"Yes," Aunt Nell said, cool as a cucumber. "She said two men were here helping you load boxes into the car. Lily didn't want to disturb you, so she just walked the horse back to Wesley's. I've brought the forty dollars we agreed upon." She rummaged around in her pocketbook and continued talking.

"I thought we could just end the matter here, but on second thought, I think you're right. I think we had better get the sheriff out here. We can't have Lily thinking that it's all right to break the law."

I gaped, openmouthed, at Aunt Nell. Whose side was she on, anyway? But Aunt Nell didn't even glance my way.

"You know, if she stole the horse, she might have stolen something else. I think I'll recommend to the sheriff that he search your place thoroughly. You know, make sure nothing else is missing."

Mr. Babcock was visibly sweating now.

"Well, now, that ain't necessary. I'm sure she didn't take nothin' else."

"Really, Mr. Babcock, I think it's in your best interest for Sheriff Geddes to make a complete search here. You might be missing something valuable and not even know it. I'll just use your telephone and call him myself."

Mr. Babcock jumped in front of Aunt Nell to block her from getting to his door.

"I said that ain't necessary. We don't need the sheriff out here."

"But, Mr. Babcock—"

"Git on with you," Mr. Babcock said, guiding Aunt Nell back toward the buggy. "Just go on home now."

"But we haven't paid you yet," Aunt Nell said.

"Keep your money. You can have the horse. Just git."

"Well, if you're sure," Aunt Nell said, climbing into the buggy. I scrambled in after her.

"I'd like to see him in jail," Aunt Nell said as we rode home. "But it was a pleasure to watch him squirm. We'll tell Sheriff Geddes about what you saw and let him handle it. I don't think Mr. Babcock will be bothering us anymore."

12

Worthless kept me busy the next few days. It's what Papa had taken to calling him. I didn't want to call him Worthless, but I hadn't thought of a good name yet and, until I did, Papa's name stuck.

If I wasn't walking Worthless, I had him standing in the water. Papa said Worthless had founder, an inflammation within the hoof walls, and the only way to save him was to soak his feet in cold water and to walk him. Papa came up once a day to check on my horse, and Aunt Nell brought me my meals there and sat with me while I ate. I even begged to sleep by the quarry so I could keep an eye on Worthless, but Papa said no, so I had to be content with spending almost every waking moment with him. I'd made Worthless sick by feeding him too much too fast. Something else that was my fault. At least I could do my best to make Worthless better.

Every evening I informed Emily about Worthless's progress. She was sincerely interested in everything I told her, and it was easier to talk to her about his condition than about hers.

Worthless spent so many hours standing in the shallow end of the quarry that it got so he'd step into the water without me tugging on him. I guess that cold water felt good on his hot, swollen feet.

On the fourth morning, Worthless nickered when he saw me. Papa felt his hooves.

"Well, the fever's out of them, and he's walking better. He may make it after all."

I hugged Papa so hard I almost toppled him backward. Papa laughed, and I realized I hadn't heard him laugh for a long time. He hugged me back, too. I couldn't have been happier if Black

Beauty himself appeared before my eyes. I'd been so afraid that Papa would never forgive me.

"Keep soaking his feet today," Papa said, "and tomorrow we'll see about getting him down to the barn."

My spirits were higher that day as I stood next to Worthless. Emily still sat heavy on my heart. I was responsible for Emily getting sick and for Worthless getting founder, but Worthless I had helped, and he was getting better. There was nothing I could do to help Emily.

By week's end, Worthless had improved enough that I was leading him on short walks around the farm. When he didn't limp anymore, I got on his back for the first time and rode him around the yard. I couldn't have been prouder if I'd been riding Black Beauty himself.

Papa watched us nervously, wondering how Worthless would act after being treated so badly, but I trusted him completely. Worthless was nothing but gentle, and even protective of me. Papa even tried hollering a little and waved a flour sack near Worthless to see if he would spook, but Worthless never batted an eyelash.

Papa said I shouldn't ride him too hard or too far, seeing as how he was still weak, so some days I didn't ride him at all. We'd walk together, me talking a blue streak. I didn't even have to lead him; Worthless followed me around like a dog. I poured my heart out to him, and he listened as no one else did. I fed him and brushed him, and in return he carried me away from the sadness and hopelessness that had settled like a fog on my family.

As Worthless got better, Emily got paler and thinner. She was wasting away. Grandma and Mama made all her favorite dishes, trying to tempt her appetite, but she hardly ate anything.

Mama continued to tell her she was getting better and that soon she would get strength back in her arms and legs, but the look on her face didn't fool me. I don't think it fooled Emily, either. I noticed Dr. Pembroke never told Emily she was getting better.

He did surprise us all one day by saying he was

going to unplug the iron lung. Mama's face paled.

"Unplug it?" she asked. "Why?"

"It will be for only a minute or two, at first," Dr. Pembroke said. "I'm hoping to force the diaphragm to work on its own, build it up so that, eventually, she'll be able to breathe without the iron lung. You willing to try it, Emily?" Emily nodded.

Dr. Pembroke warned us what to expect, but it was worse than anything we'd imagined.

As soon as the motor stopped hissing, Emily's lips turned blue, and she began gasping for air like a fish out of water. Her back arched, and her arms fluttered as she fought for air. The terror in her eyes was horrible to see.

Dr. Pembroke plugged in the iron lung. Emily's body shuddered, then began to relax as the machine took over her breathing, and all of us who'd been watching began to breathe again, too.

When Grandma stroked Emily's hair, I noticed her knuckles were white from clutching the edge of the iron lung.

"It was just the first time," Grandma said, her voice shaky. "It'll get better."

But it didn't. Each time Dr. Pembroke unplugged the iron lung, it was the same—the blue lips, the writhing body, the terror-filled eyes that begged for help. And with each failure, the desperation on Emily's face grew.

I dreaded seeing Dr. Pembroke's car pull into the yard, wanted to be somewhere else, anywhere else, just so I wouldn't have to watch Emily's face. And yet I clung to the hope that this time Emily would show some progress.

It went on for weeks, and then, one day, Dr. Pembroke popped in, exchanged a few words with Emily, and turned to leave.

"We aren't going to unplug her today?" Mama said.

"No," Dr. Pembroke said quietly. "We won't put Emily through that again."

Mama looked stunned. A chill ran through me as I understood what he was saying. There was no hope that Emily would ever leave the iron lung.

I couldn't bear to be in that room another

minute. I threw a blanket on Worthless and rode up to the quarry. Worthless walked right into the water out of habit.

It was a hot day—hotter than blue blazes, Papa would have said—and the water looked so inviting. I left Worthless standing in the shallow end and climbed up along the shore to where the lip of the rock was ten or twelve feet above the water. It made a good vantage point to look down the valley, and I could see Boyd McNeal and his boys out in their fields, loading hay onto a wagon. Thinking of the chaff from that hay made me feel itchy and hotter than ever. I'd noticed how one rock up on this cliff face jutted out a little more than the others, making a perfect diving board. I looked down the path toward our farm, but Papa was off, and it'd be awhile before Aunt Nell came bringing my dinner pail. No one would see me, except Worthless. He watched while I shucked my clothes and jumped into the water.

Maybe Emily had gotten polio from swimming in the quarry. Well, maybe I'd catch it, too. I deserved to catch polio. It would be my punishment for pushing Emily in the first place. And if I ended up in an iron lung, maybe I wouldn't feel so guilty that Emily was in one.

I had to swim to the shallow end to climb out, and I patted Worthless as I went by. I climbed up to the diving rock and jumped, this time doing a cannonball. I'd have to see if I could get Aunt Nell to do one of those. By my fifth jump, I'd completely forgotten about catching polio. I was having too much fun.

After I tired of jumping, I floated on my back and watched hawks glide by, their dark shapes silhouetted against the billowy clouds. One of the clouds looked like a horse head, and I imagined a whole herd of wild horses racing across the sky. I could almost hear them nickering to each other, and Worthless must have heard them, too, because he answered. Startled, I rolled over in time to see Worthless on the cliff face above me. He was watching me, moving his feet nervously, and it looked to me like he was getting ready to jump.

"Worthless, no! Go back!" I called, but it was too late. Worthless leaped, his feet moving as if he were galloping through the air. When he hit the water, he sent a plume of spray ten feet into the air. He came to the surface, his head held high, eyes white with fear, churning toward me. I saw then what danger I was in. If he reached me, he'd drown me. I flung myself toward shore, swimming as fast as I could, and reached dry ground a few feet ahead of Worthless. He came on land, snorting and shaking himself. He stood with his head on my shoulder, trembling, and I laughed shakily myself, patting and telling him what a good boy he was. I marveled that he had jumped in after me, as scared as he was. It touched me that he'd gotten so attached to me already, but then he'd seen little kindness before I'd come into his life.

As I stood there hugging him, a vision of King and Marlene flashed through my mind. Worthless had jumped once. Would he jump again?

I got on his back and rode him up onto the diving rock. It took only a little urging on my part to get him to leap again. As we hit the water, Worthless's head snapped back and hit me hard in the face. Tasting blood and feeling for broken bones, I realized why Marlene had jumped off King. I'd have a hard time explaining to Mama how I'd split my lip. On all the next dives, I flung myself off to the side before we hit the water.

I guess it's the innocence of youth that I never thought of it being dangerous. It only felt exhilarating to me, a glorious freedom. By the fifth jump, I'd renamed Worthless. He was Pegasus now, my wonderful flying horse.

I fairly danced home, almost bursting with excitement. I longed to tell someone about my lovely afternoon, but I was pretty sure Mama and Papa would be horrified to learn of it and might ban me from riding Pegasus altogether. Perhaps I'd tell Aunt Nell; she wouldn't tattle on me.

I heard the murmur of voices and peeked into the kitchen. Mama and Papa sat at the table, talking. Papa placed an envelope in Mama's hand.

"Mr. Findlay gave me five hundred dollars for Lady. Said he's always admired her. He promised to take good care of her."

I sagged against the doorframe. Papa had sold Lady? I couldn't believe it. Papa loved that horse.

"I'm sorry you had to sell her, Wesley," Mama said, but Papa shrugged off the words.

"No, she's only a horse. I only wish I had another one like her so I could sell her for an equal amount. Five hundred dollars. That once seemed like a fortune. Now it won't even cover our debts."

Papa laid his head back against the wall and closed his eyes.

"I feel like such a failure, Maggie," he said. "All I ever wanted to do was provide a good home for you and the girls and watch them grow up. But I wasn't able to protect Emily, and now to have to sit by and watch that machine breathe for her . . . I don't think I can bear it."

It felt like nails were being driven into my heart, hearing the anguish in Papa's voice. He was blaming himself, and I was more to blame than he. Instead of helping, I'd only caused Papa more worry what with my selfishness and stealing.

"None of this was your fault, Wesley," Mama

said. "You couldn't have kept Emily from getting polio. And you have provided a good home."

Mama leaned against Papa and held him.

"We'll get through this," she said softly. "Emily's alive, and that's all that matters. Even if we lose the farm, we'll make it as long as all of us are together."

Seconds passed before I could breathe. Lose the farm? Had it come to that? If we lost the farm, where would we go?

I slunk upstairs but was too sick at heart to sleep. I heard the clock downstairs chime one, two, three o'clock. Finally, I crept from bed and lit a candle. I took a piece of stationery from the top of my bureau and began to write.

13

I had almost forgotten that night until a morning six weeks later. All of us were eating breakfast, all of us except Mama who was spoon-feeding Emily in the living room. Dr. Pembroke had sent the nurse home. He said Mama and Grandma had become just as capable of taking care of Emily as he or the nurse could have done, and Papa and Mama didn't need the extra expense of paying for a nurse. I wished I could have been sent somewhere, anywhere, to get away from the sound of the iron lung. It filled the house night and day, constant and unrelenting. There was no escaping it; the sound burrowed into my skin. Even miles away, I could still hear it in my head like another heartbeat. Papa and Mama seemed so grateful for the iron lung because it was keeping Emily alive, but to me, it seemed to have taken everything from her. The very machine that breathed life into Emily had stilled her spirit.

Papa was ashamed he hadn't been able to pay Dr. Pembroke. Once he'd even hidden in the barn when Dr. Pembroke came just so he wouldn't have to face him, but this last time, Papa had squared his shoulders and met Dr. Pembroke in the yard.

"I'm sorry I don't have the money to pay you, Horace," Papa said, coming right to the point. "I'll pay you when I can."

"I know you will, Wesley," Dr. Pembroke said.

Papa had done all he could to raise money, but still the debts mounted. He sold some of the cows, but none of the area farmers had money either, so he'd practically given them away. He'd looked for extra work in town, but no one was hiring. He'd gone to the bank, but they'd turned him away, too. I heard him tell Mama it was only a matter of time before the bank served us eviction papers. After that, I dreaded the sound of any car in the yard.

On this particular morning, we heard the crunch of tires on the driveway. Fear flashed across Papa's eyes, and he rose quickly.

"That's probably someone from the bank," he said. My stomach gave a sickening flop. "I'll want to speak with him alone."

Aunt Nell glanced out the window.

"I don't think he's from the bank," she said. "He's come in a truck."

We followed Papa onto the porch. Large red letters on the side of the truck spelled out Drummond and Gray Circus.

The man came toward Papa, extending his hand.

"I'm Ben Jarvis," he said. "I'm here to speak to a Miss Lily Randall?" My stomach flopped again.

"That'd be my daughter here," Papa said. "What is it you wish to see her about?"

"Took awhile for her letter to catch up with me," Mr. Jarvis said. "Always on the road, you know. I'm here to see about the diving horse she wrote to me about."

Papa turned to stare at me.

"Diving horse?"

Mr. Jarvis's face registered confusion.

"Am I mistaken that you have a diving horse for sale?" he said.

I pushed past Papa.

"No, you're not mistaken," I said. "I'll show you."

Not only Mr. Jarvis followed, but Papa, Grandma, and Aunt Nell as well, puzzlement written all over their faces. I figured I was leading myself into a whole mess of trouble. Seemed like whenever trouble was afoot, it sought me out and then stuck to me like gum on a shoe. Oh, I'd have some explaining to do later.

Pegasus trotted alongside me up to the quarry and stood patiently while I clambered onto his back. I saw Papa and Grandma exchange nervous glances. Mr. Jarvis's face registered nothing.

"You wait right here," I told them, "and I'll show you what he can do."

I grabbed his mane, and Pegasus scrambled up the rocks. As we stood on top, I tasted regret, as bitter as iron, on my tongue. I was about to cross a line from which there was no return. My letter had brought Mr. Jarvis here; I was about to get the thing I'd asked for, and it would break my heart. I could still change the outcome of this afternoon. Pegasus could refuse to jump, and then Mr. Jarvis would drive away.

I bent low over Pegasus's neck and pushed those daydreams from my mind. I had to do what I could for my family. For Emily. It was time for me to grow up.

"All right, Pegasus," I whispered. "Show him you can fly."

Pegasus didn't hesitate as we leaped into the water. I jumped him again, just so Mr. Jarvis could see it wasn't a fluke. After the second time, I patted Pegasus's dripping neck. I knew he'd been flawless.

"He's not much to look at, is he?" Mr. Jarvis said. "But he's got heart, and he isn't afraid to jump. You've done a fine job training him, Mr. Randall." He pulled out his wallet.

"I'll give you five hundred dollars for him," he said, and my eyes practically dropped from their sockets. Never had I dreamed Pegasus would bring as much as Papa had gotten for Lady.

"It's Lily here who's done the training," Papa said. "And it'll be her you'll be paying."

Mr. Jarvis counted out twenty-five crisp twenty-dollar bills into my hand. Never had I seen so much money. I felt as rich as a king, with the world as my oyster. I could go anywhere, do anything, and for a whole five seconds, I imagined traveling to India or Africa or the North Pole even. Then I handed the money to Papa.

"It's for Emily," I said.

I saw Papa's hand tremble.

"Are you sure, Lily?" Papa whispered. I nodded.

"It was always for Emily," I said.

I hugged Pegasus fiercely and handed the rope to Mr. Jarvis. I won't cry, I told myself. I won't.

"Please take good care of him," I said, blinking quickly. "He's been through enough already."

Pegasus turned his head and nickered at me as Mr. Jarvis led him away. He'd learned to trust again, because of me, and now I'd betrayed him. It was all I could do not to throw Mr. Jarvis's money back at him, leap on Pegasus's back, and ride off into the hills. But I thought of Emily back in the living room, lying in her iron lung. Forever in that iron lung.

I won't cry, I thought.

"Thank you, Lily," Papa said huskily. "I think that was one of the most unselfish acts I've ever witnessed. I'm proud of you."

Oh, Papa, I wanted to ask, does growing up always hurt this much?

"This money will really help us," Papa said. "But I'm sorry you had to sell him."

I squared my shoulders.

"He's just a horse," I said, struggling to keep my voice steady. "I only wish I had another like him so I could sell him for an equal amount."

It wasn't true, and Papa knew it, but he played along. And later, when I cried myself to sleep, I found some comfort in the hope that by losing my horse, I'd saved our farm.

14

I continued to read to Emily before bed. We finished *A Passage to India* and *A Tale of Two Cities* and read some each evening from the Bible. Emily seemed to draw comfort from that and asked to hear the stories of Job and Daniel and Paul—people who'd been sorely tested.

I wasn't afraid to talk to her anymore. In fact, I looked forward to it. We'd grown close, and I was glad it was through the time we spent together and not a sense of gratitude on her part. I'd made Papa, Mama, Grandma, and Aunt Nell promise not to breathe one word about Pegasus or the five hundred dollars to Emily. It would have only made her feel bad.

I wish I could say that I would have traded places with Emily; Aunt Nell had said it, and I've no doubt Mama and Papa both would have endured the fires of hell to make Emily well, but I could not. It was like a thorn in my flesh to see her bearing up so bravely, for in truth, I knew I would never have been so accepting. I would have screamed and ranted, angry at God and life and everyone around me.

Whiskers still wouldn't come to Emily, but sometimes he sat in the doorway and watched us.

On this particular night, I had read six chapters of *Jane Eyre,* but Emily's thoughts seemed to be elsewhere, and I'd been yawning for the past hour, so I closed the book and stood.

"I guess I'll go to bed," I said. "Is there anything else I can do for you?"

Emily turned her head toward me.

"Yes, there is," she said. "You can . . . let me die."

A buzzing sound began in my head. Surely I had misunderstood her.

"What?"

"You can . . . let me die."

I laughed nervously, thinking Emily was teasing me, but in truth, I'd never seen her more serious.

"You could unplug . . . the machine one night . . . and wait, you know . . . until I am gone . . . and then plug it . . . back in . . . . No one would know." It was the most she had said since she'd gotten sick, and the effort clearly tired her.

I couldn't believe she had this all planned out.

"You'll get better," I said.

"I won't get better," she said. "If I was . . . I would have made . . . some improvement . . . by now. But I'm no better . . . I'm not going to get . . . any better. . . . And I don't want . . . to live like this."

The machine took another breath for her.

"I won't live like this," she added.

"You'll get used to it," I said weakly, hating myself for not knowing what to say, something that would sway her and convince her to keep on fighting.

Her dark eyes drilled holes into me.

"Could you?" she asked, and I wanted to weep, for I knew I could never get used to living out my days in that iron prison.

"Please, Lily," she begged.

I began to shake uncontrollably.

"I can't do it," I said, angry at my weakness and at her for asking such a thing.

"You're the only one . . . I can ask," Emily said. "Who else hates me . . . enough to do it?"

Shame spread through me.

"I don't hate you, Emily," I said, trembling violently. Even my teeth chattered. "I don't hate you."

I picked up the books and stumbled for the door, tears blurring my vision, but Emily's voice caught me before I could escape.

"If you love me, then," she said softly, "you'll do it."

15

I took pains not to be alone with Emily after
that. Mama looked at me strangely, but I turned
away each time she tried to ask me what was
wrong. Aunt Nell took over reading to Emily in
the evenings. I went about my daily chores and
helped Papa in the barn and fields, but what
Emily had asked haunted me day and night. I
could not eat or sleep. I lost weight, but so ab-
sorbed were Grandma, Mama, and Aunt Nell in
caring for Emily that scant attention was paid to
me. For once, I was glad not to be noticed, for I
could not have explained my distress.

If I'd still had Pegasus, I would have sat in his

stall, pouring out my troubles to him, but he was gone. I guess he wouldn't have given me much in the way of answers anyway. There seemed only one person I could talk to.

I knocked lightly on Aunt Nell's door. When I heard no answer, I knocked louder. Still nothing. I pushed the door open a few inches.

"Aunt Nell?" I called softly. I held my breath and heard nothing. "Aunt Nell?" I called louder. Where could she be?

Unable to sleep anyway, I sat on the windowsill and stared out into the night. The triangle of summer stars—Deneb, Vega, and Altair—was getting lower in the sky. In a few weeks, the winter constellation of Orion would be rising, chasing the summer south. Already I could feel the chill in my bones and dreaded how the weather would pen us inside and Emily's accusing eyes would follow me and break me down. Never before had the thought of winter filled me with such despair.

I heard the door creak.

"Aunt Nell?" I said.

She gave a little squeak.

"Lily, is that you?" she asked. "Goodness, you startled me."

She flipped on the light switch, and I blinked in the sudden brightness.

"What are you doing here?" Aunt Nell asked.

"I needed to talk to you," I said. "I was surprised when you weren't here."

"I just went to the privy," she said. She sat on the bed and motioned for me to sit beside her. "What did you want to talk about?"

"Emily. She doesn't want to live anymore." I couldn't bring myself to tell Aunt Nell that Emily had asked me to help her die.

Aunt Nell was silent for a few moments.

"It's all my fault!" I burst out. "If I hadn't pushed her into the quarry, she wouldn't have gotten polio."

Aunt Nell's jaw dropped.

"Have you thought that all along?" she asked. When I nodded, her shoulders sagged.

"Oh, Lily," she said. "You poor girl. You didn't cause Emily's polio."

"But I pushed her into the quarry, and she was sick the next day."

"First of all, the quarry's not a *public* swimming place." (I hadn't thought of that.) "Secondly, you and I swam there long before you pushed Emily in, and you stood in it for weeks with Worthless." (I hadn't thought of that, either.)

"Thirdly, the microorganisms that cause polio were in Emily's body for days, or maybe weeks, before she fell in the quarry," Aunt Nell said. "She didn't catch it overnight."

I wanted desperately to believe her.

"You're sure?" I asked.

"I'm sure. Dr. Pembroke will tell you the same thing. Go back to bed now," she said. "It's going to be all right."

Her words did not comfort me.

"How will it be all right?" I asked. "She's never going to get any better." I wanted her to tell me I was wrong, that Emily was getting stronger and would learn to walk again and leave the iron lung, and she'd sleep in our room again, and she'd tease me and torment me, and it would be as if nothing had ever changed, except now I would not mind her teasing. I wanted Aunt Nell to tell me this, and I wanted to believe it, if only for a moment.

Instead, Aunt Nell reached up and cradled my chin. Her hand was trembling.

"Do you trust me, Lily?" she asked.

It seemed an odd question for the circumstances, but I nodded.

"Trust in the Lord then," she said. "He hasn't forgotten you or me or Emily. He's watching over her right now. He's watching over all of us."

I knew nothing had changed, but Aunt Nell's words and touch gave me a sense of peace I had not known for many days, and I slept restfully. So restfully in fact, I did not feel Emily's spirit leave the house, for when I woke, I learned that Emily had died in the night.

16

Aunt Nell left for India soon after the funeral. "I'm angry at God," she told Grandma, "and I considered giving up being a missionary. But I've been angry with him before. That doesn't mean I can't still do his work. And maybe I can help some other children more than I did Emily."

I had hoped that Aunt Nell would take me with her, and we could grieve and heal together, but I don't know how I'd feel about Aunt Nell now, what with all these questions in my mind. Questions I'm not sure I want answers to. For you see, I have come to wonder if Aunt Nell did what Emily asked of me.

Part of me knows that I cannot possibly be right, and that Aunt Nell would never do such a thing. I mean, she's spent her whole life helping people, trying to improve their lives, but I have played the night Emily died over and over in my mind, and two things haunt me. Aunt Nell hadn't acted surprised when I told her Emily didn't want to live anymore, and Emily had died the very night that Aunt Nell and I talked. It seems too much of a coincidence, but I guess that's all it is. Even Dr. Pembroke said Emily's weak lungs and heart just gave out. Mama's always said I have too vivid an imagination.

I started back to school. The hills were changing color, and the geese were winging south—so many sights and sounds I wanted to point out to Emily. When I thought that she would never again walk with me, I could scarcely breathe.

People were kind, sending sympathy cards and bringing over food, but after a couple of weeks, their attention went on to other things, and it seemed everyone had forgotten Emily. That is one of the hardest things about losing someone, when you realize that life goes on, even without them.

Whiskers is my cat now. Sometimes he curls up on Emily's pillow and cries. Most folks wouldn't put up with all that yowling, but I understand it. Sometimes I feel like yowling, too. My childhood seems a million years behind me. My wish came true; I grew up and I am as far away from Emily as I can possibly be, and it turns out it's not what I wanted after all.

Grandma says time heals all wounds, and that we will laugh again, and right now I'm holding on to what she says for all I'm worth. Spring will come again. I will remember the good times Emily and I had together, and I will try to live a little of Emily's life for her, too. If I have a daughter, I will name her Emily. I'm going to save up so she and I can see some of the world and visit all the places Emily and I talked of going. And I will buy back Pegasus, if I can find him.

Sometimes, when I'm in the garden or the kitchen or curled up on the couch with Whiskers, I almost catch a glimpse of Emily out of the corner of my eye. It's as if she's just out of sight, just out of reach, and sometimes, when I'm up at the quarry, a cloud will pass over, and for an instant, the shadow is Pegasus leaping from the cliff.

Emily and Pegasus. The ghost pains I'll carry for life.

Natalie Kinsey-Warnock grew up on a dairy farm in Vermont's Northeast Kingdom. An avid athlete, naturalist, artist, and writer, she loves animals and has rescued most of her pets: three horses, six dogs, and seven cats.

If Wishes Were Horses was inspired by many family stories. "One of my mother's cousins had polio," says Ms. Kinsey-Warnock, "and another was a missionary in Pakistan. My mother saw the diving horses at the county fair; my grandmother's brothers managed to hitch a bull to a buggy; and the horse in the story is based on one of the horses I rescued." Beyond that, the book is "a story of family ties and the hard choices life often throws in our path."

Ms. Kinsey-Warnock is the author of numerous children's books. She and her husband, Tom, live in northern Vermont.